DOWN ON FRIENDLY ACRES

Fiddlesticks and gumdrop bars! Welcome to *"Down on Friendly Acres," a series based on the life of a real family - my family - the Friend family. My parents were farmers. They raised crops, livestock, and me, along with my two older brothers, Ronald and Duane, and a younger sister, Diane, on a farm rightly named* **Friendly Acres.**

When my father, Harold, was in fifth grade, his parents separated. When my mother, Jean, was in second grade, her father died. I believe my parents' heartbreaking moments as children made them more determined as grown-ups to provide a home where there was lots of love, joy, and peace.

Love! Joy! Peace! *Not an easy task when you have brothers and sisters running around just looking for trouble. Sometimes we stirred up trouble. Sometimes trouble just happened. In this book you'll discover a great lesson I learned growing up - the difference between accidental trouble and the stirred-up kind.*

First, one has to remember I was raised on a farm during the 1950s and 1960s. Times were very different. The word computer *wasn't even in the dictionary. That's because computers hadn't been invented yet. The word* mouse *meant a little gray varmint not a controller for a computer. The mouse pad was in the barn and getting a virus meant you could throw up any minute. Times have certainly changed.*

D0012101

What hasn't changed is man's search for more knowledge. I remember a man coming to our door to sell books - a set of encyclopedias. He told our parents, "Anything and everything your children need to know about the world is right here at their fingertips." We begged and begged our parents to get those books - the equivalent of a nice computer today. The World Book Encyclopedia *made up most of our home library. I soon discovered why my oldest brother, Ronald, was so smart. He read a lot! Some things never change.*

Duane and I were more into fussin' and fightin'. We played ball a lot in our front yard. I was very competitive. I don't recommend this, but I actually hit Duane over the head with a baseball bat. Learn from my mistakes - don't EVER do that. Listen to me! Better yet, listen to your parents.

While I'm confessing, I didn't actually call Diane "Miss Hawkephant" when we were little. However, my brothers and I do recall her special talent was learning from our mistakes. My sister rarely, if ever, got into trouble. Diane was **called** an angel.

But Grandma **is** an angel! On April 9, 2004, Grandma Brombaugh (pronounced "broomball") turned ninety-seven years young. After sharing my portrayal of her as the "wise one" in this series, Grandma handed me her journal she kept as a young single mother. This precious book contains her favorite words of wisdom that helped her walk through some difficult times. She was and still is an undercover angel in my book!

In this book you will meet up with our milk cow. As I was writing this book, I couldn't remember her name, but my father did. Our Jersey cow's registered name was Pioneer Tilly Winks Tilly. I explained to my father that in the book the cow would be a Holstein cow – black and white. He was somewhat disappointed because the reason farmers buy Jersey cows is that they give "sweeter milk and better butter!" You will soon find out the reason behind the change.

I find that one of the hardest things for parents to get right is whether or not their children accidentally or intentionally did something bad. One of the hardest things for children to do is tell the truth. It is especially difficult if the answer is "Yes, I did it on purpose." Whether you are an adult or a child, these situations require patience.

Children and sometimes grown-ups don't always have patience, but we all need patience! What's amazing is my parents never seemed to run out of patience. It didn't matter if our trouble was accidental or intentional - they always, always had patience. Grandma Brombaugh was right. My parents not only talked the talk - they walked the walk!

Let's take a walk down on Friendly Acres and... fiddlesticks and gumdrop bars... I've run out of room again. Remember,

I'M A FRIEND and U R 2!

R. Friend

DEDICATION

...In loving memory of my mother and father, Harold and Jean Friend, who not only "talked the talk" they "walked the walk"
...To my Grandma Brombaugh for her sweet spirit, contagious humor, and constant smile
...To Ronald, Duane, and Diane for having patience putting up with me as a child
...And to my husband, Bill, and my children, Jeremy and Stephanie, for their prayers, perseverance, and patience-as Chatty Cathy would say,

I love you!!!

R. FRIEND

Time Out at Home

Down on Friendly Acres #2

SUNFLOWER SEEDS PRESS

ISBN 0-9743627-1-9 Paperback
ISBN 0-9743627-4-3 Hard Cover

Text copyright © 2005 Ronda Friend
Illustrations by Bill Ross
Graphic design by Julie Wanca Design

Library of Congress Control Number 2005902599

Printed in the U.S.A.

First Printing, Second Printing, Third Printing, Fourth Printing, Fifth Printing, Sixth Printing - Sunflower Seeds Press

CONTENTS

The Friend Family

Duane, Ronda, Diane, and Ronald

CHAPTER 1

Tilly's Not-So-Sweet Surprise

Fiddlesticks and gumdrop bars! Duane swallowed a turkey - not a whole turkey - just a piece of turkey. It got all curled up and caught in his throat. The turkey won't go down and it won't come up.

This mornin' Momma and I are takin' Duane to the doctor. I hope he doesn't hafta have an operation. I don't mind if he would hafta get a shot in the arm or *you-know-where*, but not an OPERATION!

My brother's not feelin' well. Earlier this mornin' I walked into his room. Duane was tangled up from head to toe with bedcovers. All I could see was his mouth open wide like a largemouth bass. The piece of turkey danglin' from his throat swayed back 'n' forth as he yelled,

"Aaaahhhh, aaaahhhh, aaaahhhh!"

"Duane, what's wrong?"

Duane's head disappeared under the covers like a snappin' turtle! I snapped back, "Not gonna talk, Duane? Cat got your tongue? Or does a turkey have your tongue?"

Duane still didn't answer. He flipped himself over and wrapped himself tight in his bedcovers. Duane disappeared. My brother must have remembered Grandma's advice.

If you don't have anything good to say about somebody - just don't say anything at all!

"Ronda, hurry downstairs! It's time to milk the cow!" hollered Daddy.

I'll *hafta* deal with Duane later. We've a cow to milk. I flew down those stairs like Superman. Milkin' a cow is not as easy as it looks. Daddy says it takes time and lots of patience. I have lots of time but I'm still workin' on the patience.

I ran to the barn as the feeder cattle were leavin' the lot. Buford, our bull, proudly led the way. Geraldine followed. She wears a bell 'round her neck so we know when the cows come home for supper.

We raise Angus and Polled Hereford. City folk don't know the difference. But it's easy! Angus cattle are black. Polled Herefords are red with white faces and bellies.

Daddy treats his bovine (a fancy word for cow) with tender lovin' care. He reminds me of Old McDonald - except he's not old and his name's not McDonald. People call my daddy "Farmer Friend." So I decided to write a new song. Mrs. Shipley, my piano teacher, loved it.

Mr. Friend Had A Farm

R. Friend & The 96 Gang

Piano

Mist-er Friend, had a farm, called it Friend-ly Ac-res. And

on that farm he loved to dance the | barn-yard im-i-ta-tor. | Who's he watch-in' who's he watch-in

who's he watch-in' who? {

It's a cow, moo, moo! It's a cow, swish, swish! So do the
It's a cow, peck, peck! It's a chick, bawk, bawk! So do the
It's a pig, snort, snort! It's a pig, p., u! So do the
It's an owl, hoot, hoot! It's an owl, flap, flap! So do the
It's his wife, kiss, kiss! It's his wife, blink, blink! So do the

13

Daddy's not just a farmer. He's a fisherman, a veterinarian, and a weatherman. Today he's a milkman and teacher rolled into one.

We have one special cow for milkin' - a registered Holstein cow. *Registered* is a big, long word that means there's a big, long name written down on a big, long piece of paper. Our papers have her name as Pioneer Tilly Winks Tilly. We call her Tilly for short. She not only gives us milk but cream and butter for Grandma Brombaugh's yummy recipes!

As soon as Daddy plopped on the stool, his hands went a flyin'. Before you could say, *"Fiddlesticks and gumdrop bars,"* Daddy's bucket was full 'n' overflowin' with milk.

I parked myself right by Tilly Winks Tilly's udder. Then I started pullin' 'n' pullin' on those things as hard as I could. Nothin', absolutely nothin', came out! Daddy helped me wrap my hands 'round Tilly's faucets again and whispered in my ear, "Practice and patience make perfect."

Daddy let go. Minutes later there were only a few drops of milk. That's it; **I'd had it!** So I had a little talk with Miss Tilly Winks Tilly. Patience runnin' thin, I marched up to her big black and white oversized head, looked her straight in the eyeballs as she drooled drool all over my hands and overalls, lifted up her floppy ears, and declared, *"If you don't give me more milk this time, I'm gonna hafta spank you!"*

Evidently she didn't like my demands. 'Cause when I walked 'round the back of Tilly Winks Tilly, she kicked the bucket. . .

SMASH!!!

BANG!!!   OUCH!!!

What little milk was in the bucket landed on my face along with her big, black, back hoof that was covered in *you-know-what!*

I landed on my *you-know-what!* **OUCH!** It hurt.
P.U.! It stunk. I don't know what was worse - the pain
or the smell. I tried to act as though it didn't hurt.

Doctor Daddy knows daddy hugs work miracles. He hugged and cheered, "Don't tell me Ronda's running out of patience! Remember, you're a farmer's daughter and pleased as a pig in mud to be one. *Hungh, hungh, hungh!"*

Tilly made me madder than a hornet, but Daddy snortin' like a pig made me tickled pink. Holdin' back a smile, I declared, *"Tilly's out of milk and I'm out of patience!"*

Daddy assured me that Tilly had more milk. Then he taught me a lesson I'll never forget. He said, "Never, ever walk behind an animal without letting it know you're there in the first place. Always put your hand on the rump (cattle talk for bottom), and whatever you do, don't ever give up! Show Tilly who's boss."

I nodded then added, "Grandma Brombaugh always says, 'If at first you don't succeed, try, try again!' "

Daddy handed me the empty bucket. I saw it in his smile. Practice and patience make perfect! Tilly is not gonna get the upper hand this time. *I'll show her who's boss!* She's gonna *hafta* let me milk her whether she likes it or not!

I tugged 'n' pulled 'n' pulled 'n' tugged. Twenty minutes later and after squirtin' half the milk right smack dab into my eyeballs, I had milk. **I had milk!!!**

Out of breath, I bolted into the kitchen to show Momma. My oldest brother, Ronald, took one look at me and chuckled. "Why, if it isn't Tilly Winks Tilly's twin sister - *Ronda Rinks Ronda!*"

My tongue was already hangin' out from runnin' so I pointed it at Ronald. Then I whined, "Momma, Ronald called me a cow!"

Momma assured me I was not a cow. Tongue back in mouth, I boasted, "I milked Tilly, Momma! She kicked, but I've got milk. I know we're makin' homemade ice cream today for the 4-H meeting. Now I've helped!"

Momma chimed in, "Ronda! *You need help!* I'm afraid Pioneer Tilly Winks Tilly gave you a not-so-sweet surprise."

Momma handed me a mirror. I did look like Tilly's twin - *Ronda Rinks Ronda*!!!

CHAPTER 2

Ronda's Not-So-Neat Secret

My not-so-sweet surprise from Tilly was a big-old-fat black eye! "I've had it with Tilly Winks! I'm runnin' out of patience! Where's the paddle? She's gonna *hafta* get a spankin'!"

"Hold your Horses!"

After a face wash, Momma placed a bag of ice on my swollen eye as she explained, "Tilly didn't do it on purpose. I'm sure it was only an accident!"

Daddy passed through the kitchen and chuckled. "Seems like both Duane and Ronda are like accidents waiting to happen. Birds of a feather flock together. I'm amazed Ronda doesn't have a turkey caught in her throat, too."

Ronald hollered, "She would except her thumb would get in the way!"

"Momma, make Ronald take that back! I'm tryin' to stop. Somehow my big old thumb ends up in my big - I mean - my mouth when I'm upset or worried!"

Ronald interrupted, "You twirl your hair, too! You must worry a lot."

"Stop teasin' me, Ronald. I can't help but worry. Duane's in turkey trouble! We *hafta* get him to the doctor. Duane and I do our share of fussin' 'n' fightin', but deep down inside we love each other - deep as the deep blue ocean!"

"According to the *World Book Encyclopedia*, the ocean is more than six miles deep," boasted Ronald. "There's no way you love each other that much."

"Ronald and Ronda - that's enough, you two! Grandma's here," Mother instructed. "Help her with the groceries."

Grandma dropped in to baby-sit Diane and to help us make her homemade ice cream. In her bag was the secret ingredient. I'd tell you what it is, but then it wouldn't be a secret anymore!

Grandma Brombaugh knelt down for a kiss and a hug. Before she asked about my black eye, I answered, "Pioneer Tilly Winks Tilly's not-so-sweet surprise. Tilly didn't mean to do it. It was an accident."

I watched as Momma and Grandma started whisperin'. My ears aren't big enough. WHAT'S THE BIG SECRET? Where's "Miss Hawkephant," my baby sister, when I need her? Oops! There she goes playin' her favorite game - hide 'n' seek.

"Disappear, Diane! Don't you speak.
You hide and in awhile we'll seek.
Hide in the clothes hamper, behind the door,
in the closet or under the bed on the floor.
Disappear, Diane! We won't peek.
Hide yourself, you little pipsqueak."

Diane giggled. Diane disappeared.

The secret conversation was over. Momma left the room as Grandma folded her hands and looked up. I looked down at her slip - showin' again! She whispered a prayer which only proves my point. Grandma IS an angel - an undercover angel! You'd think as an angel she would pray for my big-old-fat black eye to disappear.

Grandma asked if I had eaten breakfast and then handed me a left-over deviled egg, tightly wrapped in plastic. In the meantime, Ronald pocketed peanut butter fudge from the tin can on the back porch. It didn't work this time. Grandma caught him red-handed and warned, "Ronald, you should be eating fruit or cereal - not candy. Remember, you are what you eat. Diane, ready or not, here I come!"

My eyeballs almost came out of my head! If you are what you eat, why did Grandma give ME a deviled egg? I didn't care. I was hungry, but I couldn't get the egg unwrapped. Impatient, I shouted, "Grandma, help me with this egg. I'm in a hurry. We *hafta* get Duane to the doctor. IT'S AN EMERGENCY!!!"

Grandma returned with Diane, *"the angel,"* in her arms. She helped me with my deviled egg and pleaded, "Honey, have a little patience. There's no need to worry - no need to hurry."

"Why is it grandparents never seem to hurry or worry?"

Ronald butted in. "It's because they've lived a **long, long, llllooonnngggg time.**"

Grandma added, "Long enough to know hurrying and worrying never get you anywhere."

"P.U. What's that smell?"

I hollered.

Daddy walked in with a familiar odor - pig perfume! He looked at the clock. "Ronald, it's time we get the truckload of pigs to market. Give Ronda a hug. Tell her how much you love her."

Ronald hugged me and muttered, "I love you as deep as the skin on a flea!"

Daddy asked, "What did you say, Ronald?"

With his hands over his heart, Ronald changed his tune and crooned, "I love you as deep as the deep blue sea!"

"How sweet is that!" Daddy said.

Pig stench filled the air as Daddy fiddled around in his pocket; then he disappeared. The pig perfume didn't. DOUBLE P.U.! Clothespin your nose! Momma's not gonna like havin' Daddy's overalls stinkin' up the place.

Without warnin', the strangest noise filled the air as well. Clothespin your ears! Clothespins surely come in handy around here!

Glu-glu-glu-gobble-glu-glu-glu-gobble!!!

Ronald announced, "It's a turkey - not a real one. Daddy is tryin' out his new turkey caller on Duane. He' s such a joker!"

Most of the time, Ronald is as serious as an operation. Grandma says my brother is a genius 'cause he loves to read. Daddy nicknamed him, *Mr. World BookWORM Encyclopedia.*

Ronald boasted, "A male turkey, called a tom, begins to grow red danglin' things from his throat, called wattles."

"*Wattle?*" I snickered, "*Wattle* you talkin' about?"

"Funny, so funny! Turkeys grow snoods on their foreheads."

"*A snood?*"

"A snood is like a long pointing nose."

"Pinocchio's?"

"Ronda, not as long as Pinocchio's nose, but I get your point!"

Ronald snickered, cleared his throat and continued his turkey talk! "A turkey's head turns shades of red, white and blue. Toms grow beards that grow up to five inches a year. In three years their beards can be over . . . "

Turkey talk terminated. Daddy walked by, shrugged his shoulders, and whispered in my ear, "Say a little prayer. Momma is going to need your help watching Duane. Don't let him fly the coop before his doctor's appointment!"

Fly the coop? What's that about? Now, where was I? Ronald followed Daddy out the back door like a shadow. Daddy was tryin' to cheer up Duane. It didn't work. I had a better idea. I pocketed a piece of Grandma's fudge and dashed to Duane's room. I passed Momma on the stairs. She didn't look very happy. Was it Daddy's pig p.u. or Duane's turkey trouble?

Fiddlesticks and gumdrop bars! Those bad thoughts are back! I didn't mind if Duane got a small shot in the arm or even a shot in the *you-know-where* with a huge, long needle, but not an *OPERATION!*

I opened the door, took one look at Duane, and a lightbulb went off in my head. You are what you eat. *You are what you eat.* **YOU ARE WHAT YOU EAT!!!**

"oooooOH NOooooo!!!!"

I slammed the door shut, ran downstairs, and burst through the front door. *Fiddlesticks and gumdrop bars!* Daddy's gone. But I know he knows Duane's secret too - *birds of a feather - the turkey caller - fly the coop!* Daddy should have done something. He's a veterinarian! I *hafta* keep Duane's secret a secret. Daddy's countin' on me to take care of Momma and Duane.

I didn't want Grandma to worry, too! What am I thinkin'? Grandma is too old to worry. Besides, her mission as an angel is to keep other people from worryin'. Most likely Grandma already knows my secret - I mean Duane's secret. He can't help it. Poor Duane is an accident waitin' to happen!

"Wonda! Wanna pway hide 'n' sneak?"

Diane's *babblin'* again! Now is not a good time. She's really tryin' my patience. My fingers flopped in my hair. I started twirlin' as fast as I could. I'm not tellin' anybody my secret - not even "Miss Hawkephant." Diane tugged on my overalls and pleaded again, *"Wonda, wanna pway hide 'n' sneak?"*

"OK, OK! Disappear, Diane! Don't you speak.
You hide and in awhile we'll seek.
Hide in the clothes hamper, behind the door,
in the closet or under the bed on the floor.
Disappear, Diane! We won't peek.
Hide somewhere, you little pipsqueak."

Diane giggled. Diane disappeared.

"Ready or not - here I come!"

I found my fudge-faced sister on the back porch. After cleanin' up the evidence of her misbehavior, I snuck a piece of fudge myself while Diane disappeared - *again.*

CHAPTER 3

I'm Not a Fiend – I'm a FRIEND!

Fiddlesticks and gumdrop bars! I forgot to introduce myself. My name is Ronda, R-O-N-D-A, without an "h." Every Rhonda I know spells her name with an "h." But not me, I'm different. That's what Duane says. Daddy calls me special.

My last name is Friend. F-R-I-E-N-D. I know what you're thinkin'. I made it all up. Some folks think that. It's as if they've never, ever heard the word *friend*. Some people must be plain hard of hearin' on account of they think my last name is fiend. F-I-E-N-D. FIEND! MY FOOT!

Grandma checked with Noah - not the guy with the BIG BOAT, but Noah Webster - the guy with the BIG BOOK - Noah Webster's *Dictionary*.

fiend / **'fEnd** / *noun* / a person causing mischief or annoyance / b : a person of great wickedness

Accordin' to Grandma, "wicked" is when someone plans something bad on purpose to happen to someone else. That person is mean and they mean for something bad to happen. I don't know any mean people. But I've seen one on TV. Once a year on a Sunday night my family watches *The Wizard of Oz* - everybody but Diane. She's too little and it's too scary!

I love Dorothy. She's sweet. I pretend to be her sometimes. I even wear red shoes 'cause I love her so much. Although my shoes don't sparkle.

Now where was I? Oh, yeah! The Wicked Witch of the West in *The Wizard of Oz* scares me. Her face scares me, her voice scares me, even her laugh scares me. Now SHE IS WICKED! I may not behave every hour of every day or every second in every minute, BUT I AM NOT WICKED!

"*Fiddlesticks and gumdrop bars*, Grandma, maybe I am wicked! Remember this mornin'? I ate a deviled egg and you said, 'Ronda, you are what you eat!' "

Grandma snickered. "Darling, I was explaining to Ronald the importance of eating fruits and. . . "

"You don't understand. Earlier in my mind I was thinkin' it would be neat if Duane would *hafta* get a shot in the arm or *you-know-where* with a needle. Now that's downright mean!"

Grandma agreed. She asked if I planned on purpose for something awful to happen. I told her, "I may not be an angel, but I didn't mean to be mean! Sometimes bad ideas pop into my head."

Grandma warned me not to let those bad thoughts stay too long then added, "And besides, you're a friend. According to Noah one little letter can make a big difference."

friend / **'frend** / *noun* / 1 a: one attached to another by affection or esteem / b: Acquaintance / 2 a: one that is not hostile

In Grandma's own words *hostile* means "mean." Enemies are mean people. I AM NOT MEAN - at least not most of the time. I AM NOT HOSTILE - not every day. I AM NOT WICKED! I don't even like the sound of that word! I AM NOT A FIEND. Give me an "R!"

F-R-I-E-N-D! I'M A FRIEND.

I told Grandma, "I'd rather be a *friend* than a *fiend*. From now on if someone messes up my name, I'll say, 'My name is Friend - opposite of enemy. You spell my name F-R-I-E-N-D!' I'll be a friend to everyone!"

"Everyone, Ronda? There's no better place to start than by being a friend to your brother, Duane. Besides you two are a lot alike. Birds of a feather flock together!"

*Birds of a feather? **BIRDS! FEATHERS!*** Grandma knows, too. She knows Duane's turnin' into a turkey! My head started poundin'. My secret was tryin' to escape! I wrapped a bandana 'round my head and mumbled, *"Mbmlblbmm???"*

Grandma lifted my bandana, smiled, and asked, "Ronda, are you hiding something?"

You can't keep secrets from an angel very long. I whispered, "Do you promise not to tell? Duane's turnin' into a . . ."

"HELP! hELP ME!!! HELP!"

Grandma muttered, "I wonder what's ruffling up Duane's feathers?"

Grandma flew up the stairs like she had wings to help Duane!

Birds? And Wings!?! And Feathers!?!?
OH, My!!!
Birds? And Wings!?! And Feathers!?!?
OH, My!!!

CHAPTER 4

Unfortunate Events

I removed the bandana and attached clothespins to my ears, nose, and mouth instead. One can't be too careful with secrets. Calm and smilin' from ear to ear, Grandma reappeared out of nowhere - another sign of angelhood. Before I could ask about Duane, she asked, "What's wrong, Ronda?"

"Mlblbmmmbmlblbmmm!"

Grandma gently removed my clothespins.

There was a slight chance Grandma didn't know my secret. I fumbled 'round for something to say. "Grandma, Daddy always says Duane and I are like accidents waitin' to happen. What does he mean by accident?"

"Let's check with Noah Webster."

---

ac·ci·dent / 'ak-s&-d&nt, -"dent; 'aks-d&nt / *noun* / 2 a: an unfortunate event resulting especially from carelessness or ignorance

---

That's it! Duane has an unfortunate event happenin' in his life. *He's turnin' into a turkey!* It's up to me to keep it a secret - even from an angel. Maybe Duane does need a shot in the *you-know-where* to keep him from turnin' into a turkey.

So Grandma wouldn't think I had something up my sleeve, I changed the subject. "Grandma Brombaugh, I thought this whole mean thing over and I am mean. I don't mean to be mean. *It's - it's - it's an accident!*"

Grandma replied, "Accidents happen. Intentions are planned. Both require patience. The fact is we don't plan accidents, Ronda. But when accidents happen, it's how we react that counts. This story will help you understand the difference between accidental trouble and the stirred-up kind. When your mother was five, she accidentally went to sleep with gum in her mouth. Next morning the gum was stuck to the ends of her beautiful, long, brown hair. Tears streamed down your mother's rosy, red cheeks as she came running into the kitchen."

"What did you do?"

"We tried getting the gum out with ice, but it was impossible. Rocked and cradled in your Grandpa's lap, I heard him sing to your mother,

'Fiddlesticks and gumdrop bars, doesn't matter where you are. Accidents happen - don't come unglued, just smile. It's all in your attitude!'"

"Grandpa Brombaugh pulled out his best scissors from the drawer, plopped a bowl on top of your momma's head, and snipped away. Moments later she had a new do!"

"She loved it! A few hugs and a couple kisses later, all her tears dried up. A bigger-than-Bozo smiley face appeared!"

"*Fiddlesticks and gumdrop bars!*" I exlaimed. "*When life gives you lemons . . .*"

". . . *make lemonade,*" Grandma finished. "So you see, Ronda, people don't plan accidents. Accidents happen. Duane didn't plan on getting a piece of turkey stuck in his throat . . . ."

"Pioneer Tilly Winks Tilly didn't plan on givin' me a black eye . . . ."

". . . and your momma didn't plan on getting gum stuck in her hair. They're all accidents. There's nothing we can do except to respond to accidents with patience."

"Grandma, patience isn't very easy!" I added.

"No, it's not. Patience is a waiting game. Duane has to wait to get the piece of turkey out of his throat, you have to wait for your black eye to go away, and your momma had to wait for her hair to grow back. Always remember, patience is the best remedy for any trouble. And according to Noah,"

remedy / 1: a medicine, application, or treatment that relieves or cures a disease / **2:** something that corrects an evil

"Grandma, what different kinds of remedies are there?"

"Remedies can be lots of things - medicine, a new hairdo, an ice pack, a hug, Band-aids, songs, or cookies. No matter what the remedy for every trouble we might face, we always. . ."

". . . *hafta* have patience. Grandma, what was that other thing you mentioned - something about *indentions?*"

"*Intentions.*" Grandma giggled. "But you'll have to wait because it's time to stir up a batch of oatmeal cookies."

"Eat cookies before lunch?"

"Ronda, you know the rules. Besides, this recipe calls for patience. The cookie dough needs to be chilled at least one hour before we bake them. "

"Even cookies take patience? Besides, Grandma, your refrigerated oatmeal cookies are well worth the wait!"

Grandma Brombaugh's Refrigerated Oatmeal Cookies

1 1/2 CUPS QUICK OATS	3/4 CUP SIFTED FLOUR
1/2 TSP. SODA	1/2 CUP BUTTER
1/2 TSP. SALT	1 EGG
1/2 CUP BROWN SUGAR	1/2 CUP WHITE SUGAR

1 TSP. VANILLA

COCONUT, CHOCOLATE CHIPS
OR RAISINS TO TASTE

DIRECTIONS: Sift dry ingredients. Cream butter and add sugar. Blend well, then add egg and vanilla. Beat again. Add dry ingredients and mix well. Chill several hours. Practice patience and wait. Roll dough into small balls. Bake on ungreased cookie sheet 10-12 minutes in a 375 degree oven. Makes 2 1/2 dozen.

CHAPTER 5

Fiddlesticks and Gumdrop Bars!

The phone rang. Momma looked disappointed. The doctor couldn't see Duane for another couple of hours. I patted her on the back and smiled. "Don't worry! Didn't Grandma Brombaugh teach you patience is the best remedy for any trouble? We'll just *hafta* wait!"

Momma grinned.

"Grandma told me your gummy hair story," I went on. "But she didn't tell me what I really want to know. When I get excited, or if I'm tryin' to figure out a problem, or if I don't want to say a bad word, I shout, *'Fiddlesticks and gumdrop bars!'* Why?"

"Let's write a poem while we're waiting." Momma suggested. "When we're finished, you'll know the secret about fiddlesticks and gumdrop bars!"

SECRET? Momma thinks she's the only one with a secret! I positioned my bandana and clothespins. Momma took one look at me, raised her eyebrows, and asked, "What's up with you?"

I *hafta* keep my secret! Fingers crossed on one hand, I fanned the air with the other, took a big whiff of air and exclaimed, "P.U.!!! I can still smell those plump piggies goin' to market."

Stinky poo, stinky poo, stinky poo poo!

Momma sniffed, smiled, and set the timer.

Fiddlesticks & Gumdrop Bars!

Big black eye, my name is Ronda,
No "h" and yes, I don't ride a Honda.
I'm six years old - feelin' just fine,
Off to my grandparents - I rise and shine.

Down in the valley and over the creek-
on their farm for one wonderful week.
Through the dense woods, up and over the hills.
Dandelions, wildflowers, and daffodils.

Grandma's MeMa with rosy red cheeks,
Gray hair in a bun - she's quiet and meek.
Grandpa's Boompop - plump with no hair,
Eyes of sky blue, he hugs like a bear.

Grandparents are special, somewhat sublime,
I think it's because they've lived a long time.
They're not in a hurry, you can sit on their laps,
What amazes me most is they love to take naps!!!

Went down by the pond with our fishing gear,
Cast my pole in the air - hit MeMa in the rear.
The hook in her bottom, there went my rig-
Boompop plucked it out and MeMa did a jig.

Singing, "Fiddlesticks and gumdrop bars!
It doesn't matter where you are.
Accidents happen, don't come unglued,
Just smile, it's all in your attitude."

Sat down for dinner, I said, "Please pass the jelly."
Boompop let the bowl slip - it plopped on his belly.
I waited to see what their reaction would be,
They both started to laugh, then burst out in glee.

Singing, "Fiddlesticks and gumdrop bars!
It doesn't matter where you are.
Accidents happen, don't come unglued,
Just smile, it's all in your attitude."

They hung a picture later that night,
MeMa dropped the hammer - not a pretty sight.
It landed on top of Boompop's toe,
To my surprise they began to do-si-do.

Singing, "Fiddlesticks and gumdrop bars.
It doesn't . . .

BBBBUUUUUZZZZZ!

Momma shut the timer off.

"What a silly poem about accidents, Momma. But I still don't know what fiddlesticks and gum . . ."

"Sweetie, keep your shirt on. My secret won't be a secret for long. We'll finish our poem later."

Momma went to get Duane. I'm not the only one who needs to keep my shirt on. *Fiddlesticks and gumdrop bars!* I've got a secret, too -

a not-so-nice secret!!!

CHAPTER 6

Beard, Snood, & Wattle

Totally exhausted from playin' hide 'n' seek with Diane, Grandma plopped down on the kitchen chair. I was exhausted from tryin' to keep my secret. I thought, *If anybody could keep a secret, it would be an angel.* So I went for it.

"I was thinkin' about how *'we are what we eat,'* and how Daddy always says, *'Duane and Ronda are like accidents waitin' to happen'* and Noah says, *'Accidents are unfortunate events resulting from carelessness or ignorance,'* and I have come to a conclusion. The piece of turkey has been stuck in Duane's throat sooooo long . . ."

Grandma interrupted, ". . . soooooo long you think Duane is turning into a turkey?"

"YES! YES! **AND MORE YESSES!** Duane is a turkey - *a RED, WHITE, AND BLUE BEARDED TURKEY!* I knew you knew! But, Grandma, not only that, he's growin' a bushy beard. He has a long snood (kind of like Pinocchio) and to top it all off, Duane has a big, enormous red wattle. *Wattle* we do?"

Grandma Brombaugh patted me on the back, shook her head, and muttered, "Let me see your nose, Ronda. Remind me never, ever to let you have left-over deviled eggs for break . . ."

"Wah, wah, **wah!**"

Diane looked like she'd seen a monster or worse- a huge overgrown turkey! Cryin' like the baby she is, she was playin' hide 'n' seek again. We just forgot to seek. Grandma wrapped her up in her wings - I mean arms.

My baby sister is the *"Hawkephant"* in the family. She watches me with her big, bright, brown eyes, listens with her enormous elephant ears, and records with her busybody, baby brain what-not-to-do. Babies never get into trouble. Diane doesn't even have a time-out chair!

Now where was I? Grandma didn't seem to be worried one bit about Duane. She promised Diane they would make hats today. Hats? *Fiddlesticks and gumdrop bars!* It's true. Diane is becomin' an angel!!! She's growin' a halo. And Grandma wants to cover it up with a hat.

Speakin' of hats, Duane appeared in the kitchen doorway with a huge red, white, and blue hat on his head, a red scarf 'round his mouth and neck, and Daddy's winter jacket. His body was tremblin' like a worm before it's put on a hook, his two enormous eyes were about to pop out of his head, and he was scratchin' his arms and legs like a mad monkey throwin' a temper tantrum.

Duane acted *weird*. Momma looked *worried*. Diane seemed *scared*. Grandma looked like an *angel*. And me - I looked like a *black-eyed bandit!!!*

Momma instructed, "Let's go to the car. We need to hurry or we'll be late."

I ran upstairs and grabbed my favorite doll, Chatty Cathy.

As we were leavin', Grandma hollered, "Jean Vivian, don't hurry and don't worry!"

Momma drove 'n' drove 'n' drove. Duane was constantly scratchin' his arms and legs. I guess growin' feathers and a beard would drive anybody crazy. Frustrated, Duane asked, *"Are we there yet?"*

"Almost, Duane. It won't be long now!"

Two seconds later, I asked, "Momma, how much longer until we get to the doctor's office?"

Momma chuckled. "Let's have fun and play the waiting game. Remember, Ronda, patience is the best remedy for trouble. And, besides, we'll get there when we get there!"

I thought to myself, *Of course, we'll get there when we get there. I just hope we get there before the cows come home!*

What seemed like hours later, I forgot everything Grandma taught me about patience and blurted out for the tenth time,

"ARE WE THERE YET?"

CHAPTER 7

The Patient Screams!

HIP-HIP-HOORAY! We're at the doctor's office. There's no more waitin'. It's a good thing I wore my bandana. Doctors' offices smell weird! Momma explained to me that the smell kills the germs. I could see why. To take my mind off the smell, Chatty Cathy and I looked at magazines until we were both *bored stiff*, especially Chatty Cathy!

"What are we doin' here?" I asked.

Momma explained that this was the "waiting" room. With my bandana lifted, I commented, "No wonder it's called the 'waiting room,' that's all we've done is wait. We've been waitin' 'n' waitin' 'n' waitin' in this doctor's office. I think we should move to the doctor's waitin' room and let him know we're waitin' in his waitin' room for him and we can't wait to be waited on - so hurry up! Let's get this show on the road!"

"Ronda, calm down. Have some patience," Momma advised as she patted me on the shoulder.

"Why should I have *patience?* Duane's the *patient* here. Besides, if there is ever somebody with lots of *patience,* it should be a doctor. And if he doesn't wait on his *patients* soon, he won't have any *patients* - and neither will I - *patience,* that is. I'm not the doctor!"

The nurse stuck her head through the small window and said, "Excuse me, the doctor is running late. He appreciates your patience."

I thought to myself, *I hope he appreciates his patients, too!*

Momma still looked worried, which made me worried. "Ronda Jean, take the thumb out of your mouth, stop twirling your hair, and take that bandana off your face!"

I obeyed; then I whispered in Momma's ear, "I haven't seen Duane's face all mornin' - just the inside of his mouth. It looked normal - as normal as the inside of a mouth can look with a piece of turkey curled up hangin' down between his tonsils and that little flapper thing. Duane is totally covered up and squirmin' like a slitherin' snake tryin' to shed its skin. He's hidin' something."

Momma assured me everything was just fine. I wasn't convinced.

Fine, My Foot!!!

Fine, Duane's Turkey Foot!!!

Duane's wearin' a winter coat, a scarf and hat in the springtime. There's definitely something up his sleeves! Gobbled up by a gigantic book, he started jumpin' up 'n' down, actin' like a turkey-in-the-box. Now I just knew something was fishy on account of the book was upside down! I tried to calm myself down by askin' Momma the name of our doctor.

Momma replied, "It's Dr. Daryl B. Payne."

My eyes got as big as saucers. Extremely loud in my thoughts, so Duane couldn't hear, I shouted,

DOCTOR THERE'LL BE PAIN!!!!!

Finally, the doctor was ready. Momma guided Duane as the nurse led us back a long hall to a teeny, tiny room without windows. She closed the door.

Momma had me close my eyes while she helped my brother get into a hospital gown. I placed my hands over Chatty Cathy's eyes, too! *Hospital gown?* Momma reassured me that Duane wasn't gonna *hafta* go to the hospital.

When I finally could open my eyes, Duane was sittin' on a table, totally covered up with sheets, readin' his gigantic book. He looked like a mummy - *a mummified turkey!* Momma explained we were now waitin' in the "examining" room.

Dr. Payne walked in as I asked, "What's the 'examinin' room?"

"Sweetheart, the examining room is where I look to see what's wrong with someone," Dr. Payne answered.

I thought to myself, *If you ask me, it doesn't take a tree full of owls to figure out what's wrong with Duane.*

All of a sudden I took a giant breath and blurted out my thoughts, breathin' only twice. *(First breath)* "So, **DR. THERE'LL BE PAIN,** (sorry, Duane) I'm only six but I know what's wrong. Duane has a piece of turkey caught in his throat. It won't go down and it won't come up. I told him, 'You're gonna *hafta* swallow your pride and your turkey, too.' We tried the bread and water trick. It didn't work. I patted him hard on the back while he stood on his head upside down - that didn't work either. Grandma Brombaugh, the undercover angel, says, 'You are what you eat.' I figure the turkey has been stuck in his mouth for almost a day." *(Second breath)* "Mind you, it's an accident and accordin' to Noah, an accident is an unfortunate event resulting from carelessness or ignorance. Duane's unfortunate event - he's turnin' into a turkey - **BEARD, SNOOD, & WATTLE.** *Wattle* we do? All I can say is that you have your work *cut out* for you. *OOPS!* I hope that doesn't involve a *knife*. What are you waitin' on? We've been waitin' a long, long time; and I think we have been very, very, VERY, **PATIENT!**"

I sighed and waited in silence until Dr. Payne seemed to echo,

"Well! WELL!!! WELL!?!?!"

"Is that a question?" I spoke up. "If so, I am well - except for my big, black eye Pioneer Tilly Winks Tilly gave me this mornin'. I'm absolutely normal. Duane's the one who's sick, and unless you can do something quick, he'll be turnin' into a . . ."

Mother squeezed my knee and whispered, "Ronda, that's enough. Now close your mouth."

"And, Duane, why don't you open yours," Dr. Daryl B. Payne instructed as he unwrapped my mummified brother.

We all gasped for air! The turkey in the throat was the least of my brother's worries. Duane was covered from head to toe in big red . . .

DOTS &
SPOTS &
MORE DOTS!

Dr. Daryl B. Payne quickly explained, "Duane, in medical terms, you have a bad case of *urticaria!*"

"URTICARIA!" I spoke up again. "If you ask me, it looks as though he ran into a beehive and stayed for supper!"

Dr. Payne patted my head, chuckled, and explained, "Chatty, I mean Ronda, Duane wasn't stung by bees, but he does have hives. Hives is the common name for *urticaria.* Some people break out in hives when they become nervous or anxious."

The doctor continued, "Duane, in all my years of practicing medicine, I've never seen a body break out in so many bumps. You've been worrying way too much about the turkey stuck in your throat. I can assure you, you don't have chicken pox – not even 'turkey' pox. And don't be nervous. There's a remedy for your 'worry warts' – a little medicine and a little time. As for the turkey, my dentist friend next door can fix you right up."

Dr. Payne handed Momma a prescription. He asked me and Chatty Cathy to wait outside. I didn't understand until . . .

"Aaaauuuugggghhhh!!!!!"

Uh, oh! Duane got his remedy in the *you-know-where!* At least he didn't *hafta* have an operation.

Fiddlesticks and gumdrop bars! We sat in another waitin' room waitin' some more! Still scratchin', Duane preferred standin'. I closed my eyes and saw Grandma Brombaugh prayin', "Thank You for teaching Ronda patience today. Amen."

After waitin' 'n' waitin' 'n' waitin' until we thought we couldn't wait anymore, another nurse led us to another examinin' room. There was a huge, black chair bolted to the floor. The nurse smiled and placed a fluffy pillow on it. Duane gently sat down and the chair immediately went up.

While the nurse attached an oversized napkin with a chain 'round my brother's neck, the chair was still goin' up. She stopped the chair just in time. His head was about to hit the ceilin'! Duane didn't need any more troubles. Dozens of metal instruments were lined up on a shiny table. Could it mean an operation, after all?

Duane was not smilin'.

Two taps on the door and a thin, tall man in a long, white jacket appeared. His crocodile, shiny-white smile scared me. And by the look on his face, we scared him, too! He rolled his eyes, cleared his throat three times, and with a raspy voice spoke, "You must be Chatty Cathy, and you must be the boy with the turkey in his throat. Do I have the remedy for you. I'm Dr. Smiley. I'll have you smiling in no time."

Duane was not smilin'.

In his hands Dr. Smiley held a huge straw hooked to a very large machine by a long cord. With his foot he pressed down on a pedal. The machine growled like a giant vacuum cleaner.

Duane was not smilin'.

Dr. Smiley instructed Duane to open his mouth big and wide. I interrupted. "Excuse me, Dr. Smiley. Didn't your momma tell you never, ever put something down someone's throat?"

Momma was not smilin'.

Dr. Smiley chuckled. Momma whispered something to the doctor and then assured me everything was just fine.

Duane still was not smilin'.

Dr. Smiley continued as the straw disappeared into Duane's mouth. The human vacuum cleaner roared. Moments later a piece of turkey emerged, stuck to the end. Duane's remedy for his turkey trouble took two more rounds of vacuumin'. Duane's dilemma was over - *no more turkey.*

Duane smiled! Dr. Smiley smiled. Momma smiled. I smiled and then danced with Chatty Cathy and sang,

"FIDDLESTICKS AND GUMDROP BARS!
Accidents happen, don't come unglued - smile, it's all in your attitude!"

CHAPTER 8

We Scream for Ice Cream!

By the time we got home, the cows were home, too. Daddy was feedin' his bovine beauties their supper. I burst through the front door and found Grandma Brombaugh hidin' under the kitchen table. Diane's runnin' 'round with her new homemade hat, screamin,' *"Weady or not - here I kum!"*

Grandma placed her finger to her lips. It was too late! Grandma's **IT**. With her slip showin' again, she crawled out from under the kitchen table and asked, "How's our patient?"

I announced, "Duane is NOT a turkey! We played the waitin' game and found out he has hives but not from bein' by a beehive. His bumpy hives all over his body are like worry warts caused by thinkin' too much about the turkey thing."

"I knew it!" exclaimed Grandma.

I thought to myself, *I knew she knew - she's an angel!*

Momma added, "With a little help from the doctors, a little medicine, and a little more patience, Duane's troubles will soon be over!"

"*Patience is the best remedy for trouble . . .*" Grandma winked and then added, "and ice cream is a close second!"

Ice cream makin' is not only a family tradition - it's a family affair. Grandma gets things started. Then I add the secret ingredient to the mixture already on the stove. My arm almost falls off stirrin' 'n' stirrin' till every piece melts. We wait for the mixture to cool. Then we place it in the metal container and add Tilly's contribution - fresh milk 'n' cream.

Momma positions the wooden paddle (not the kind that hurts but the kind of paddle that turns the mixture inside the container into ice cream). Then the container is taken outside on the back porch and placed inside the wooden barrel.

The crank is positioned on top of the wooden barrel. Daddy dumps ice in between the container and the barrel while Momma pours rock salt on the ice. This process continues as *Mr. World BookWORM Encyclopedia* explains how ice and salt work together to freeze the mixture into ice cream.

Daddy, head ice cream maker, warns us to be patient and never be tempted to peek inside. If rock salt gets into the mixture, it would never freeze. He jokes, "If that happened, we'd be eating *soup cream* - not *ice cream.*"

Diane goes first. She turns the metal handle 'round 'n' 'round as the container spins 'round 'n' 'round, which makes the ice spin 'round 'n' 'round. Her turn lasts about thirty seconds. *"Miss Hawkephant"* flies the coop and hides again.

I'm next. While I'm crankin', I close my eyes to dream, about eatin' the ice cream, and in my dream my arm is about to fall off. So I quit. Duane takes over until it gets hard to crank. Then Ronald cranks 'n' cranks until it gets even harder to crank. That's when Daddy steps in. When he can't crank it anymore, it's ready!

Daddy takes the metal container to the kitchen sink where Momma wipes off all the salt. She removes the top and there's the *yummy ice cream.* The paddle comes out slowly as she scrapes off most of the ice cream. Meanwhile, Daddy puts the ice cream in the freezer for the 4-H meetin' while Momma holds the paddle, which is covered with ice cream, over a plate.

This time, makin' ice cream was different. Lightbulbs flashed on 'n' off in my head as I jumped up 'n' down. *"Fiddlesticks and gumdrop bars!"* I shouted. "Don't you get it? The trouble we go to makin' ice cream helps us *practice patience.*"

With six set of eyes starin' at me, I explained, "We milk Tilly, which by itself takes lots of patience, and we *wait* for the cream to rise to the top of the milk. We mix all the ingredients and even *wait* for the secret ingredient to melt. Then we *wait* for that mixture to cool. We *wait* to take our turn, and then we *wait* for the ice cream to harden. But in the end this whole waitin' game is worth the trouble and the *wait!*"

Grandma was all aglow - maybe it was just her halo! Then she added, "But always remember, it's the times when we find ourselves in trouble that we need patience the most."

I added, "And no matter what, *patience is the best remedy for any trouble!*"

"Ice cream is a close second!" Daddy hollered. "Who wants the paddle?"

Normally nobody - *I mean NOBODY* in his right mind wants the paddle - except now. Spoons in our hands, we Friends all scream,

"I scream, you scream,
we all scream for ice cream!"

CHAPTER 9

(Time) Out at Home

4-H meetings start at 6:30, but all the kids come early to play ball. I'm too young to be in 4-H, but they let me play anyway. I *love* baseball! I *love* to win! I *love* the pressure of bein' up to bat. Especially tonight 'cause I was the winnin' run. But I *didn't love* what happened next!

"RONDA JEAN FRIEND!"

Oops! You know what that spells.

T-R-O-U-B-L-E! **TROUBLE!** T-R-O-U-B-L-E

And this time I was the only one in it. Momma grabbed my hand. I looked back at Duane lyin' out cold on home plate and screamed, *"What a dingbat!"*

That was not a good idea. With that said, Momma stepped up the pace. I had a hard time keepin' up with her. Headed for my time-out chair again, I cried, *"Momma, it was an accident - **an accident waitin' to happen!**"*

"Ronda Jean, this was **NO** accident," she said as she showed me the broken bat.

"I didn't mean for the bat to break! I meant, I didn't mean to be mean and hit my broth..."

"Miss Hawkephant" appeared out of thin air. *"Wonda did it on porpoise."*

"Diane, I didn't do it on porpoise."

"Momma, I thaw it wif my big bround eyes. Wonda did it on porpoise!"

"No, Diane. I didn't do it on porpoise. *I did it on purpose - not porpo - oops!"*

Momma chimed in, "So you *did* do it on purpose."

What was I thinkin? "Oops! OK. I guess you can say I just ran out of patience. Momma, I'm sorry."

Momma sat me down and didn't even take the time to tell me, "DON'T YOU MOVE!!!"

She dashed back outside with a bag of ice for Duane's head. Then I pointed to myself and shouted, "DON'T YOU MOVE!"

I didn't. I just sat in my teeny, tiny corner thinkin' of how much I love baseball. My family loves baseball. Our favorite team to watch is the Cincinnati Reds. My favorite baseball song is "Take Me Out to the Ball Game." You're supposed to stretch seven times when you sing it!

How can I be in trouble over baseball?

T-R-O-U-B-L-E.

Trouble?

Fiddlesticks and gumdrop bars! When we find ourselves in trouble, that's when we need patience the most! Patience is a waitin' game. That's it! I'll use my time-out time and a terrific tune to tell my tale of trouble!

♪ TAKE ME OUT TO THE BALL FIELD!!!

Take me out to the ball field.
Last inning, two outs - I'm at bat.
Dad gently throws me a strike down the pike!
I swing strong and the ball takes a hike!
A grounder rips down the third baseline.
Duane lunges, leaps lickety-split!
1 - 2 - 3 - hops the ball right into my brother's mitt!

But, wait, this story's not over.
The force knocked Duane flat on his back!
I'm roundin' second - opportunity knocks.
Duane's down for the count - I don't stop!
Head down, my feet now are spinnin'.
Slip by third - Duane's out like a light.
But 1 - 2 - he opens his eyes, smiles
and then his feet take flight!

We both head for home in a fury!
The winner's first one to home plate.
When out of the blue darts the bull from the barn!
What's goin' on - someone sound the alarm!
Buford is headed straight toward us!
With manners I yell, "Duane, go first."
1 - 2 - Duane gets me out - 'cause on home plate
he landed headfirst.

That's 'cause Buford took Duane for a free ride!
High in the sky he did fly!
Duane beats me to home - he tags me out!
I pick up the bat and start to shout!
Oh, Duane, you think you are something!
Your team has won - you're ahead!
Watch as one - **big bump** appears
on your forehead!

Dingbat!

As soon as I finished my song, Momma entered the room and I blurted out, *"I'm sorry, I'm really, really, REALLY sorry!"*

I even added a couple sniffles! But it wasn't workin'.

"Sweetheart, sometimes saying sorry is not enough. You could have really hurt Duane. Fortunately, he's going to be OK. But what if he had to go to the hospital for a real operation? What you did was no accident. *It was intentional.*"

Sniffles and more sniffles, I continued. "Momma, there's that word again – *indentions.* What are indentions?"

"*Intentions*, darling. Intentions."

Out came Noah's big book.

---

in·ten·tion·al / in-'tench-n&l, -'ten(t)-sh&-n&l / *adjective* **1** : done by <u>intention</u> or design : <u>INTENDED</u> <intentional damage> synonym see <u>VOLUNTARY</u>

Momma added, "Intentions are planned - done on purpose. There are bad and good intentions. Take, for example, your favorite movie, *The Wizard of Oz.* Dorothy had good intentions. The Wicked Witch of the West had bad intentions. Bad intentions - the stirred-up kind of trouble - will get you into trouble every time."

Momma kept goin'. "Ronda, you wanted to get back at your brother because he tagged you out at home. It's so important to *wait and think* before you *speak and do*. Now you have an opportunity to practice patience. Take time to decide what it will take to make it right with your brother."

Momma left. *Miss Hawkephant* didn't. I asked, "Diane, wanna pway hide 'n' sneak? You hide and I'll seek you **in about a day 'n' a half!**"

Diane kept smilin' 'n' starin', smilin' 'n' starin'. I stared back. I didn't blink at all. What would she ever do without me? Someday I'll take the credit when she turns her hawk wings in for angel ones. That's when I realized Diane has big, beautiful, brown eyes! OK, my baby sister is a real *cutie patootie* - hidin' 'n' spyin' here, there, 'n' everywhere. What would I do if something ever happened to her?

Fiddlesticks and gumdrop bars!

Something bad almost happened to Duane on account of me! I felt miserable. A couple of real tears fell from my eyeballs, down my cheek, and into my mouth. I love my family with all my heart - deeper than the deep blue ocean! I blinked. Then the lightbulb in my head started blinkin', too!

Little Miss Ronda - no "h" or no Honda!
Here in time-out once again.
Along came a "spyster" - sat down beside her!
What a surprise - it's Diane!

Lessons learned before she could walk;
Diane's never in trouble - she never squawks!
Those big brown eyes watch me like a hawk;
Her elephant ears listen more than she talks.

God gave us one mouth, two ears, and two eyes.
So talk less - listen more - I can be wise!
Wise like a "hawkephant" - are you stark ravin' mad?
OK, wise like my grandma, my mom, and my dad.

Accidents happen, intentions are planned.
My brain is spinnin' - now I understand!
It is all my fault. I am to blame.
No accidents here - Duane won the ball game!

I've learned my lesson - I was all wrong.
Duane's right when he says I'm a ding-dong!
I'll tell him, "I'm sorry - I'm a dingbat!"
I'll ask forgiveness, then make him a hat!

Time's up for time-out!

I had plenty of time to *wait 'n' think*. Now it's time to *speak 'n' do*. I wiped the tears from my eyes, whipped up my surprise, snatched a cookie and glass of milk, and headed upstairs.

Duane, wearin' only swimmin' trunks, was sittin' on a huge, fluffy pillow in the middle of the bedroom, readin' a book for real this time. The book was right side up! His body was plastered with pink lotion - another part of the remedy.

Duane lowered his book. **OH, NO!** Duane looked like our terrier dogs with a sunburn. Teeny 'n' Tiny and now Duane have rings around their eyeballs. Evidently the blow to the head with my bat gave Duane a *big, black eye, too!*

I admitted, "I guess birds of a feather do flock together. I'm Pioneer Tilly Winks Tilly's twin - *Ronda Rinks Ronda* - the Holstein cow look-alike. And you're Teeny 'n' Tiny's Terrier twin - *Duany Deeny Diny* - the toy terrier look-alike."

We both laughed.

"Duany Deeny Diny, what a great athlete you are to be able to get me out at home. You must have had a blast flyin' in the air when Buford took you for a ride."

"It was awesome until I landed on my *you-know-what!*"

I felt a glow as I crammed a cookie into my mouth and took a big sip of ice cold milk. Then, I swallowed. I cleared my throat and apologized, "Duane, I want you to know I'm so sorry. What happened today was all my fault. I'm to blame. You have my permission to call me a 'dingbat'!"

He did.

"Ronda Winks Ronda
is a dingbat,
a dingbat, a dingbat!
Ronda Winks Ronda
is a dingbat,
a ding-ding bat!"

"OK, OK.
That's enough!"

We smiled and gave each other a high five. Duane closed his eyes while I placed his surprise on his head. I laughed till I snorted.

Hungh!
Hungh! Hungh!

With his eyes wide open, Duane laughed so hard that his pink lotion cracked up! I handed Duane a mirror. We were so funny-lookin' the mirror broke. I guess you can say it cracked up, too!

CHAPTER 10

Hafta Have Patience

With Chatty Cathy tucked in my arms, I listened as Momma started our bedtime chat. Momma shared, "Ronda, today's been tough because learning to be patient isn't easy for children or adults. I thought you might like hearing Noah's definition of patience."

PATIENT: **1 pa·tient / Pronunciation: 'pA-sh&nt /** 1: bearing pains or trials calmly or without complaint

---

"That's me!" shouted a familiar voice from under the bed.

It wasn't Diane. She was fast asleep in her own bed. It was Duane. His body leaned to one side as he carefully sat down on top of the bed. We laughed. Momma agreed. "Duane, you have been a *very, very, patient patient* today with your *turkey trouble, shots, shiners, and spots.*"

Daddy appeared in the doorway, laughin'. "Birds of a feather do flock together! Both of you have learned a valuable lesson on patience today!"

All the while knowin' Duane did a better job of not complainin' than I did today, I shouted, "You can say that again!"

Daddy began to say, "Both of you have learned a valuable . . ."

Momma smiled. "Your daddy is quite the joker! Ronda and Duane, tonight instead of reading a book, let's talk about why we need patience. Let's come up with ten reasons we *hafta* have patience."

I shouted, "That's easy, Momma!"

I jumped out of bed, put on my pair of red shoes, and planted myself under the light in the middle of my room. With motions and emotions, I danced and sang:

"Milkin' cows, black eyes,
hide 'n' seek, Diane's cries,
Doctor visits, like it or not,
waitin' rooms, long needle shots.
When Duane wins fair 'n' square,
ice cream makin', time-out chairs!
We all need patience, everyone.
Whether six years old or ninety-one!"

My audience applauded as they grinned from ear to ear. What I had to do next was one of the hardest things I've ever done in my life. I took a big breath, *swallowed my pride,* and shared more of my thoughts from my troubled time in time-out.

"Duane, I want you to know I'm not a 'Hawkephant,' but I was watchin' you and I'll always remember today. Unlike me, you practiced patience without complainin'."

At that point I had everyone's undivided attention so I decided to go for it. In one breath I blurted out some more of my time-out thoughts.

"Duane, you slept with a piece of turkey ticklin' your throat and then your body broke out in *bumpity bump bumps* all over your skin. My baseball bat and I added a few more *bumpity bump bumps* to your forehead. Then Buford and Dr. Daryl B. Payne added a few more *bumpity bump bumps* to your already *bumpity bump bumped body*. And like it or lump it, I gave you a shiner. That's more than enough to drive someone crazy. But never once did I hear you complain. Duane, you've shown me what havin' patience is all about. I am proud to be your sister and I'm proud to be your friend - not your fiend!"

"My *fiend*? What's that?"

"Let's just say a fiend is wicked - like the Wicked Witch of the West in *The Wizard of Oz*. She scares me!"

"She scares me, too!" Duane confessed.

Not to be outdone, Duane in one breath continued, "I'd like to take the credit for taking everything so well, but the turkey in my throat was bothering me so much I could hardly talk. I was *soooo* scared and worried about all the worry warts all over my body, I didn't want to talk about it. And when you hit me over the head with the baseball bat, I was out like a light. When I came to, you were already in time-out, which was a good thing for you."

"Why so?" I asked.

"Because I would probably have given you your second black eye. But having to wait gave me time to think of all the trouble I would have been in. At that point I realized I had more than my share of trouble for one day."

"Momma, our two birds of a feather have both grown up a lot. Time for a group kiss and a hug and a love around the neck," Daddy shared.

We all joined in for our group hug except for Duane - too much pink lotion. I prayed and then pulled Chatty Cathy's string in hopes she would say the right thing! She did.

"I'm sorry! I'm sorry!"

Duane waved and went to his room. I crawled into bed, shoes and all. Momma asked me to take my red shoes off. I begged, "Pretty please, sugar and honey, can I keep them on just for tonight? I want to remind myself even though my troubles started when Duane tagged me *out at home* and I hit him *out at home* and then went to *time-out at home* that there's still . . . (I paused to click my heels together three times) . . . *no place like home! There's no place like home! **There's no place like home!**"*

Momma smiled and agreed, "OK, but just for tonight!"

"Momma, will I ever outgrow needin' patience?"

"I'm afraid not," Momma replied. "Everyone, everyday, everywhere needs patience. *Children* need patience. *Grown-ups* need patience! *Doctors* need patience. . . ."

". . . and patients," Daddy chuckled and added, "The older you get, the more you'll realize how important patience is whether your troubles are accidental or intentional."

Out came two humongous yawns, and I groggily muttered, "Thanks for havin' patience with me today. Thanks for havin' patience with me tomorrow and the next day and the day after that and . . . I'm sleepy. I love . . .!"

"We love you, too!" Momma added, "Ronda, don't you want to know my sweet secret about fiddlesticks and gumdrop bars?"

"I'm reeeaaalllly sleepy. I might hafta . . ."

Zzzzzzzz . . . Zzzzzzzz . . . Zzzzzzzz

". . . *hafta* wait patiently to discover Momma's sweet secret."

Momma and Daddy gave each other *goo-goo eyes*, turned the lights off, then walked away arm in arm. They were singin', *"Fiddlesticks and gumdrop bars, Ronda still doesn't know what they are. . ."*

THE END

P.S. Next mornin' I woke up dreamin' . . .

Fiddlesticks and gumdrop bars!

(Wattle you waitin' on? Turn the page!)

What's Momma's sweet secret? I flew downstairs —
Superman! Everybody seemed to be playin' hide 'n' seek
but *nobody was hidin', nobody was smilin', and everybody
was seekin'.* I asked, "What's goin' on?"

Momma's voice shook. *"We can't find Diane!*
Ronda, check upstairs!"

I stumbled upstairs. The only thing I saw was
a humongous heap of bedcovers stacked high on her
bed. I checked the closets, behind the doors, under the
bed, and everywhere. I started twirlin' my hair and my
thumb plopped in my mouth. *Where's Diane? What
would I do if something ever happened to her?*

*You'll hafta have patience
and wait to read the next book to find out!*

*Keep your eyes peeled
and look for the sunflowers!
Every full illustration in this book
has a sunflower hidden in the page.*

Happy hunting!

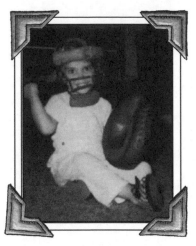

"Take me out to the
ball game!" Ronda

Here's Chatty Cathy &
Ronda, and Diane

"Get into the car!"
Momma as a baby!

"That's a bowl haircut!"
Momma

"There's no place like home!"

"I scream for ice cream!"
Duane & Ronald

"I love you"
Ronda & Diane

Fiddlesticks & Gumdrop Bars

slap your knee,   clap your hands,   jam-bo-ree!

Fid - dle Fad - dle Fid - dle Fad - dle   Fid-dle Fad-dle Foe   Fid - dle Fad-dle Fid - dle Fad-dle,
Fid - dle Fad - dle Fid - dle Fad - dle   Fid-dle Fad-dle Fee   Fid - dle Fad-dle Fid - dle Fad - dle

do - si - do!   Clap your hands   touch your nose,   Fid - dle Fad - dle Fid - dle Fad - dle
Jam - bo - ree   Clap Your hands,   Slap Your knees   Fid - dle Fad - dle Fid - dle Fad - dle

Fid - dle Fad - dle Foe
Fid - dle Fad - dle Fee

© 2005 Sunflower Seeds Press

GRANDMA BROMBAUGH'S
HOMEMADE ICE CREAM

6 eggs   2 1/2 C. sugar   2 C. milk

Beat up eggs, add milk and sugar then cut up 14 large marsh-
mallows (secret ingredient) and cook until they dissolve.
Cook on medium heat and don't over cook!
Let stand to cool and then add:

1/2 pt. whipping cream

1 pt. of half and half

5 C. milk   6 t. vanilla

Place into an electric ice cream maker or for a fun family event
place into an old fashioned crank ice cream maker
and crank away!

GRANDMBA BROMBAUGH'S
REFRIGERATED OATMEAL
COOKIES

1 1/2 C. quick oats   1/2 C. white sugar
3/4 C. sifted flour   1/2 C. brown sugar
1/2 C. butter   1/2 tsp soda
1/2 tsp salt   1/2 tsp vanilla   1 egg

Coconut, Chocolate chips, or raisins to taste

Grandma
Brombaugh

Directions

Sift dry ingredients. Cream butter, add sugar. Blend
well. Add egg, vanilla, beat again. Add dry ingredients
and mix well. Chill several hours. Practice patience and
wait. Roll dough into small balls. Bake on ungreased
cookie sheet 10-12 minutes in a 375 degree oven. Makes
two and one half dozen.

Check Out Our Websites

Children's Website
www.DownonFriendlyAcres.com

Songs! Games! Pictures! Contests!

Enter the "Friend of R. Friend's Author Contest!"
Enter the "Funniest Farmer's Tale."
Email your clothespin picture.
And much more!

Educator's and Parent's Website
www.SunflowerSeedsPress.com

Order "Down on Friendly Acres" series through our websites!

"R. Friend – Swallows Her Pride" #1 (forgiveness)
"R. Friend – Time Out at Home" #2 (patience)
"R. Friend – Hats Off to Heroes" #3 (kindness)
"R. Friend – Panic in the PigPen!" #4 (perseverance)
"R. Friend – Woolly Baaad Lies" #5 (honesty)

Besides Grandma Brombaugh, What Do Other People Say About Patience?

"Patience is the ability to count down before you blast off."
Author Unknown

"A hot-tempered person starts fights;
a cool-tempered person stops them." *Proverb*

"Patience is the companion of wisdom." *St. Augustine*

"Nothing gives one person so much advantage over another as
to remain always cool and unruffled under all circumstances."
Thomas Jefferson

"The key to everything is patience. You get the chicken by hatching
the egg, not by smashing it." *Arnold H. Glasgow*

"If you are patient in a moment of anger, you will escape a hundred
days of sorrow." *Proverb*

"The two most powerful warriors are patience and time."
Leo Tolstoy

"Like farmers we need to learn that we cannot sow and reap the
same day." *Anonymous*

"Slow and steady wins the race." *Aesop*

"Patience and diligence, like faith, remove mountains."
William Penn

"How poor are they who have not patience!
What wound did ever heal but by degrees." *Shakespeare*

According to Noah . . .

Patient -bearing pains or trials calmly or without complaint,
not hasty, steadfast despite opposition, difficulty, or adversity;
able or willing to bear

Patience - the capacity, habit, or fact of being patient

About the Author

Photo: Bob Fitzpenn

Ronda Friend (R. Friend) is a master storyteller, musician, singer, songwriter and motivational speaker. She has captivated the hearts of hundreds of thousands of children. Administrators, teachers, parents and children describe her presentations and books as "heart-warming, energizing, hilarious, fun, sensitive, caring, entertaining and refreshing."

As author of the *Down on Friendly Acres* series, Ronda's vision is to plant seeds of a different kind – seeds of kindness, patience, laughter, perseverance and honesty into the lives of children and their families. *Woolly Baaad Lies* is the fifth book in her farm series. Her *Wild & Wacky Animal Tales* series of picture books include *P.U. You Stink!* (teamwork) and *Waddle I Do Without You!* (friendship), slated for release in 2011.

Ronda holds a B.A. degree in education with a minor in music. She has two grown children, Jeremy and Stephanie, and lives with her husband, Bill, in Franklin, Tennessee.

Check out www.RondaFriend.com for booking information.

Remember . . .
Grandma Brombaugh says,

*"Patience is the best remedy
for any trouble!"*